ADVENTURES at
TABBY TOWERS

Raintree is an imprint of Capstone Global Library Limited, a company incorporated in England and Wales having its registered office at 264 Banbury Road, Oxford, OX2 7DY – Registered company number: 6695582

www.raintree.co.uk
myorders@raintree.co.uk

Edited by Jill Kalz
Designed by Heidi Thompson
Original illustrations @ Capstone Global Library LImited 2018
Illustrated by Deborah Melmon
Production by Kathy McColley
Originated by Capstone Global Library
Printed and bound in China

ISBN 978 1 474 74881 0
21 20 19 18 17
10 9 8 7 6 5 4 3 2 1

British Library Cataloguing in Publication Data
A full catalogue record for this book is available from the British Library.

Disappearing Darcy

by Shelley Swanson Sateren
illustrated by Deborah Melmon

CONTENTS

ADVENTURES at TABBY TOWERS

IT'S TIME FOR YOUR ADVENTURE AT TABBY TOWERS!

At Tabby Towers, we give cats the royal treatment. We are a first-class cats-only hotel that promises a safe, fun stay for all guests.

Tabby Towers has many cat toys and games. We make personal play time for every guest. And we have a large indoor kitty playground that will satisfy every cat instinct, including climbing and hunting. Also, your kitty will never tire of watching our cow and chickens from the big playground window.

We are always just a short walk away from the cats. Tabby Towers is located in a large, sunny, heated room at the back of our farmhouse. Every cat has a private litter box and a private, three-level "apartment", complete with bed, toys and dishes. Of course, we will follow your feeding schedule too.

TABBY TOWERS
WHO'S WHO

KIT FELINUS

Kit Felinus (fee-LEE-nus) is a lifelong cat lover.
She has worked for cat rescue and shelter
operations much of her adult life. After seeing the
great success of Hound Hotel — the dog hotel next
door — she realized the need for a cat hotel in the
area. So she started Tabby Towers. She now cares
for cats all day long and couldn't be happier!

TOM FELINUS

Tom Felinus is certain that his wife, Kit, fell in love
with him because of his last name, which means
"cat-like". He is a retired builder. He built Tabby
Towers' kitty apartments, cat trees and scratching
posts. He built the playground equipment too,
which will keep your kitty happy for hours.

TABITHA CATARINA FELINUS
(TABBY CAT, FOR SHORT)

Tabby Cat is Kit and Tom's granddaughter and a
true cat lover. In fact, the cat hotel is named after
her! She helps at Tabby Towers in summer. The
8-year-old daughter of two vets, Tabby lives in
the city and has her own cat. She's read almost
as many books about cats as her grandma has!
Tabby will give your kitty all the extra attention or
playtime he or she may need.

Next time your family
goes on holiday, bring
your cat to Tabby Towers.

Your kitty is sure to have
a purr-fect time!

CHAPTER 1
Hundreds of cat heroes

I'm Tabitha Catarina — Tabby Cat, for short.
I L-O-V-E, love cats. Hairballs and all. Cats are
my favourite animals in the world. I even have
a cat of my own. She's a beautiful Himalayan
cat called Bootsie.

Last spring, my parents gave me a choice.
They said I could spend the whole summer
on a big film set with them or stay with my
grandma Kit and grandpa Tom at their farm.

(My mum and dad are vets. They care for animals that appear in films. That's their job.)

I decided against the film set. There weren't going to be any cat actors there, only horses. I chose to spend the summer with Grandma Kit and Grandpa Tom. They're true cat lovers, like me. In fact, they run a cat hotel on their farm. It's called Tabby Towers. So when I stay with them, I get to work and play with cats seven days a week!

I'm *such* a lucky girl.

There *is* a problem, though. And her name is Alfreeda Wolfe. Alfreeda is a girl my age who lives on the farm next door to my grandparents' place. She wants to be good friends with me, but sometimes she can be *so* annoying.

See, Alfreeda L-O-V-E-S, loves dogs. That's okay, except she *brags* about them. All. The. Time. She puts down cats a lot too.

One day last month, she said there were hardly any cat heroes in the world. She acted like every dog was born wearing superhero clothes. She even said a caring, brave cat called Darcy wasn't a hero. (Darcy was a guest at Tabby Towers that day.) Alfreeda said that cats are too selfish to do great things – even Darcy.

Well! That certainly made my "claws" come out. Do you think a "cat fight" broke out? Get cozy, and I'll tell you all about it.

🐾 🐾 🐾

It was the middle of June, on a warm, rainy morning. Alfreeda, Grandma Kit and I were in my grandparents' living room. We were getting ready for a magic show.

The show was going to start at four o'clock, right there in that big room. Lots of people had said they'd come. I was going to be the magician. I even had an amazing costume.

My sweet cat, Bootsie, was going to help with the tricks. Bootsie is a super-calm cat. She doesn't mind a room full of strangers. I knew she'd do a great job.

I'd already painted the inside of the Magic Disappearing Box black. (Grandpa Tom had built it.) Now I covered a small table with a red cloth. I set three metal cups upside down on the table and hid a tiny metal bell under one of the cups.

"I know that trick," said Alfreeda. She was busy painting the outside of the Magic Disappearing Box. "You show Bootsie where the bell is. You cover the bell with a cup. Then you move all the cups around. She watches while you move them, right?"

"Yeah," I said. "Bootsie's really good at this trick. She tracks the bell with her eyes. And ears. No matter how many times I move the cups, she touches the right cup with her paw when I stop."

"A lot of *dogs* are great at that trick," said Alfreeda. "They do a super job, especially when you put a treat under the cup. A *dog's* sense of smell is much more powerful than a cat's."

I wanted to say, "You've only been here fifteen minutes, and you're *already* bragging about dogs?" But I kept my mouth shut. Grandma Kit was giving me "the look". She gave me that warning look a lot when Alfreeda was around. It meant, *Tabitha, be nice. We're neighbours.*

"You girls are my heroes for putting on this fundraiser," Grandma Kit said. She sat on the sofa, sewing a button on my costume. "I love that the magic-show money will go to the cat shelter. Lots of homeless cats will be helped because of you two."

"Oh, I'm not a hero," said Alfreeda. "This fundraiser was Tabby Cat's idea, after all."

"But you're helping so much," Grandma Kit said. "You're making Bootsie's disappearing box look so . . . magical. Look at those stars!"

"Thanks," Alfreeda said, beaming.

Grandma Kit was right. Alfreeda was a great artist. I really needed her skills for the magic show. But I didn't need to hear her talk about dogs today.

Grandma Kit stood up and hung my costume on a hanger. "That's done," she said. "Tabitha, we have a new hotel guest coming soon, a ragdoll cat called Darcy. Please let me know when he gets here."

"Okay," I said.

Grandma Kit headed through the kitchen towards Tabby Towers, at the back of the house.

I began to set up a ticket-sales table by the front door. "I can't wait to meet Darcy," I said.

Alfreeda laughed. "I don't get it," she said. "What's a ragdoll cat? You mean, a floppy, stuffed doll that looks like a cat?"

I shook my head. "Darcy's not a toy," I said. "A ragdoll is a type of cat. They're born being able to do a special trick. They go limp in your arms when you hold them – just like a rag doll. Their bones seem to melt like butter."

Alfreeda laughed again. "You're kidding me," she said.

"No," I said. "Just wait. You'll see."

I set up rows of chairs at the far end of the big room. Alfreeda painted more stars on the disappearing box.

"Maybe we are a little hero-like," Alfreeda said. "But you know who the *real* heroes are?"

I rolled my eyes. I knew exactly what she was going to say next.

"*Dogs*," she said. "There are *so* many dog heroes in the world. They save people's lives all the time. They pull people from raging fires.

They pull them from deep water. They find people in snowstorms. They save them from deadly snakes, from alligators . . ."

Mm-hmm. And there was more.

"But cats?" she said, waving her paintbrush in the air like a magic wand. "You never hear about cats saving people's lives. Do you? Cats don't do great things. Know why? Because cats are selfish. They care only about themselves."

"That's *not* true!" I cried. "There are *hundreds* of cat heroes!"

I really wanted to give Alfreeda a long list of cat-hero stories to prove her wrong. But I was so cross, I couldn't think of one story.

That's when the doorbell rang.

I frowned at Alfreeda and marched across the room. I threw open the front door and forced myself to smile.

"Hi!" I said to a very sad-looking woman holding a cat carrier. "Welcome to Tabby Towers. My name's Tabby. Please, come in!"

CHAPTER 2

Sad news about Joy

The woman stepped into the living room. "Good morning," she said. "I'm Ms Jackson. I'm dropping off our cat, Darcy."

A man and a girl were waiting in the car outside. The girl covered her face with her hands. Her shoulders shook.

"Is everything all right?" I asked Ms Jackson.

"Not right now," she said. "But it will be. We're headed to the hospital. Our daughter, Joy, has to get her heart mended."

"I'm sorry," I said. "Will she be okay?"

"Oh, yes," said Ms Jackson. "But Joy's terribly sad that Darcy can't be with her at the hospital. Darcy and Joy are best friends."

I nodded. "My cat, Bootsie, and I are best friends too," I said. I kneeled down and looked through the carrier's door. "Wow," I exclaimed. "Darcy, you are beautiful."

"Thank you," said Ms Jackson, smiling for the first time. "He's a good cat."

Darcy was a large cat with a round face. He had big blue eyes, a pink nose and a little pink mouth. His long, fluffy hair was almost all white. There was just a bit of grey on his face, ears and tail.

"I've read a lot about ragdoll cats," I said. "Does Darcy really get all floppy when you hold him?"

"Yes, he does," Ms Jackson said.

"Weird," Alfreeda said, standing behind me. "Why do they do that?"

"No one knows for sure," Ms Jackson said. "That floppiness makes ragdolls extra special. Some of them do stop acting floppy as they get older though."

"Can I hold him?" I asked.

"Of course," Ms Jackson said. "Darcy is very relaxed, even around new people. But first, would you please tell Kit we're here? We are in a bit of a hurry."

"Sure," I said. "I'll be right back."

I ran into the kitchen and opened the door beside the refrigerator. It led to Tabby Towers. My grandparents had turned their big family room into the cat hotel. I opened the door just a crack so no kitties could leap out. Guests at Tabby Towers had to stay in the hotel at all times. Safety first!

"Grandma Kit?" I called. "Ms Jackson's here with Darcy!"

"I'll be there in a minute," she called. "Right after I get the cats into their apartments."

A row of kitty apartments lined one wall in Tabby Towers. Grandpa Tom had built them.

Each one was a little three-level unit. We never left the guests outside their apartments if we weren't there to watch them.

I hurried back to the living room and couldn't believe my eyes. *Alfreeda* was holding Darcy. Alfreeda! That made my hair stand on end, like the fur on an angry cat. *I* wanted to hold him first!

"He's so heavy," Alfreeda said.

"Ragdolls are big cats," Ms Jackson said. "They're strong too."

"And he *is* floppy," Alfreeda said. "It's like he has no bones at all."

I crossed the room and ran my fingers through Darcy's hair. It was *so* soft. Petting him made some of my anger melt away.

Grandma Kit came in and gave Ms Jackson a hug. "Hi, Annie," she said. "Good to see you.

I'm sure all will go well at the hospital. And don't worry about Darcy. We'll take good care of him while he's here."

"Thank you," Ms Jackson said. "Being apart from Joy will be hard for him too, I'm sure. They're together all the time, night and day."

"I'm not surprised," said Grandma Kit. "Ragdolls are great with children."

"We'll give Darcy lots of love," I promised.

"Thank you, dear," Ms Jackson said. "We'll see you again in a few days." She kissed Darcy and left.

"Let me hold him now," I told Alfreeda.

"Sure thing, Tabby Cat," she said, putting Darcy in my arms.

"Wow," I said. "You *are* one big, floppy ragdoll, Darcy boy. A handsome one too."

Alfreeda watched the Jacksons' car leave the driveway. "I know Joy from school," she said. "She's a year behind me. I didn't know she was unwell. I wonder what's wrong with her."

"Her heart isn't working like it should," said Grandma Kit. "It's beating too fast. The operation will fix it, we hope."

My own heart beat a little faster just thinking about it.

"That sounds really scary," Alfreeda said. "It's too bad Darcy isn't a dog. A *dog* would make Joy feel better. A cat couldn't care less if its owner is sick."

My mouth dropped open. My fingers spread far apart, and my fingernails seemed to grow into claws. I wanted to shout, "That's *not* true!" Why couldn't Alfreeda just take all her dog talk and *go home*?

CHAPTER 3

Crying for J-O-Y

I think Grandma Kit could see I was about to say something unkind. She took my arm and led me towards Tabby Towers.

"I think you'd be surprised, Alfreeda," she said in a cheerful voice. "Cats can be quite loving too. Now, let's all get Darcy settled, shall we?"

I took some deep breaths and tried to calm down. I wanted to talk to Grandma Kit about Alfreeda – *alone*. But Alfreeda followed us right into the cat hotel, like an annoying puppy that wouldn't stop annoying me.

I put Darcy in the middle of the indoor kitty playground. "Look at all the fun things," I said. "Cat trees and ladders to climb . . . a kitty highway that you can zoom around on by the ceiling . . . a kitty swing and see-saw . . . lots of scratching posts too. Time will fly by. You'll be with J-O-Y again before you know it!"

I knew better than to say Joy's name out loud. But Darcy seemed to be a very smart cat. The second I said "J-O-Y," he started to cry. Not quiet, little meows either. They were loud, high-pitched cries, one after another.

And Darcy didn't want to play with any toys. He started to walk around the room really quickly. He looked behind the cat trees, behind the see-saw, behind a plant, behind Grandpa Tom's rocking chair . . .

"Oh dear," Grandma Kit said. "He's searching for his lost friend."

"J-O-Y?" I mouthed.

She nodded. "Some cats get very upset when their person leaves," she said. "How on Earth are we going to cheer him up and keep him happy while he's here?"

I watched Darcy search for Joy. I listened to his super-sad meowing. I felt worse for him by the second.

Then I had an idea.

"I know what might cheer him up," I said, snapping my fingers. "Come here, Darcy. I have something to show you."

⇒CHAPTER 4⇐
Darcy the star

I picked up Darcy and carried him back to the living room. Alfreeda and Grandma Kit followed.

I set him down next to the star-covered Magic Disappearing Box.

"Look, buddy," I said. "We're having a magic show today. My cat, Bootsie, was going to fool the crowd in this trick box. But you can take her place. You'll be the *star*!"

Darcy hung his head and meowed sadly. He didn't even look at the box.

"I think that's a wonderful idea, Tabitha," Grandma Kit said. "It will help take his mind off you-know-who. I'll lock the front door. Don't open any doors until Darcy is back in the hotel," she warned. "I'll block Scruffy's door too. If you need me, I'll be in the hotel."

"Thanks, Grandma Kit," I said.

Scruffy was Grandma Kit's indoor-outdoor cat. He had a small door in the kitchen that led to the farmyard. He was the only cat at Tabby Towers that was allowed to go outside.

I heard Grandma Kit push a heavy basket of potatoes across the kitchen floor. She always used it to block Scruffy's door when she wanted to keep him inside.

"Okay, buddy," I said to Darcy. "This is how the box works. We open the little purple curtain in the front, like this. We put *you* inside the box, like this."

I placed Darcy gently inside. He stared at the black wall, then at the black ceiling.

"The inside is painted all black to fool the people watching," I explained in a soft voice.

He's acting so calm, I thought. *Terrific! My plan's working!*

"See how far away the chairs are?" I asked him. "That's on purpose. The people watching can't tell that the 'wall' behind you isn't wood. It's black cloth."

"Meow," Darcy said. He really seemed to be listening to me and forgetting about Joy.

"So, what you do is this," I went on. "During the act, I'll put you inside the box. I'll close the curtain in front. Then you crawl *behind* the black cloth, okay? There are some kitty treats in the secret space back there. You'll hide there, enjoying your treats. I'll wave my arms around and say some magic words. Then I'll open the curtain, and no one will see you. They'll believe you disappeared!"

"Meow," Darcy said.

I grinned. "I'm so glad you want to be the star," I said. "Are you ready to practise the trick?"

"Meow," he said.

"Great," I said. "Okay. Here goes."

I closed the purple curtain and held my breath. Darcy began to cry. Loud, sad cries.

I sighed. "He's just missing you-know-who *so* much," I said.

Alfreeda rolled her eyes. She was busy painting a sign. *ENJOY THE SHOW,* it said.

"He's just scared to be in the dark box," she said. "That's all it is, Tabby Cat. Really. Unlike *dogs,* cats don't miss people that much.

Cats aren't social animals. Dogs are. Cats only care about themselves. That's a fact."

"That's *not* true!" I snapped.

Alfreeda acted as if she hadn't heard me. "But I bet Joy is really missing Darcy. It must be scary and lonely in that hospital without him, don't you think?"

Thinking about Joy made me less cross at Alfreeda. "Yeah," I said. "Too bad Darcy can't be there with her."

The crying went on and on.

"He won't fool anyone," Alfreeda said. "Even if he's hidden behind the cloth wall. He's far too noisy."

"Just give him a minute," I said. "He'll get used to it."

But Darcy kept on crying.

"I'm taking him out of there," Alfreeda said, marching towards the magic box. On the way, her shoe bumped a small paint can and knocked it over. Paint splashed on the floor.

"Yikes!" I said, jumping up. I ran to the bathroom, grabbed an old towel and ran back to wipe up the mess.

Alfreeda had found a box of tissues and was trying to help.

"Sorry about that," she said.

"No problem," I said.

That's when I noticed the room had become strangely quiet.

"Darcy's stopped crying," I whispered to Alfreeda. "See? He'll fool the crowd, after all."

"Good job, Darcy," Alfreeda said, pushing the purple curtain open. "You can come out now."

Darcy didn't make a sound. Not even the tip of his tail showed.

"Well, this trick will *wow* the crowd," I said. "It really seems like he disappeared."

"I know!" Alfreeda said.

"Come on out, Darcy," I said. "We'll give you more treats for doing such a good job."

I lifted the cloth.

"Oh no! He's not here," I said. "He didn't eat the treats either. Where *is* he?"

Alfreeda and I stared at each other. I'd never seen her eyes so wide.

"Do you believe in magic?" she asked.

"I'm not sure," I said. "Do you?"

Alfreeda shrugged. "Maybe he jumped out of the box when you left the room," she said.

"I wasn't watching. I was wiping the floor, trying to clean up the paint mess."

I looked around the living room, high and low. My face felt hot. "Oh, Darcy," I called in a singsong voice. "Where *are* you?"

CHAPTER 5
He's not here

"Come here, Darcy," I said, dropping to my knees. "Where's our good boy?"

I started crawling around the living room to look for him. So did Alfreeda.

Together, we looked under, around and behind all the furniture. We kept calling, "Come out, Darcy!"

We searched everywhere in the living room. "He's not here," I said, my heart beating faster. "How can he not be here?"

I jumped up and ran to the kitchen. Alfreeda followed right behind me.

"Oh no!" I cried.

The basket of potatoes had been pushed away from the cat door. I ran over and kneeled in front of the little door. "Look," I said, my heart pounding.

A bit of white cat fur was caught in the opening. Darcy's fur!

"Grandma Kit!" I shouted. "Grandma Kit! Come here, quickly!"

🐾 🐾 🐾

There was a storm outside, so Grandma Kit, Alfreeda and I threw on our raincoats and boots and ran across the farmyard, towards my grandparents' barn. The rain fell hard, slapping my hood.

Grandpa Tom was in the barn. He was fixing the tractor. Grandma Kit told him that Darcy had escaped. "We thought maybe he came in here," she said.

"No sign of him," Grandpa Tom said. "Scruffy is right over there, sitting on top of that hay bale. If Darcy had come into Scruffy's barn, there would've been a terrible cat fight."

"Please come inside, Tom," Grandma Kit said. "I need you to watch the cats in the hotel while we search for Darcy."

"Of course," Grandpa Tom said, wiping oil off his hands.

"The girls and I will search the farmyard," Grandma Kit said. "If we can't find Darcy here, we'll take the truck. We'll check the roads heading towards town. It's not unusual for cats to walk many kilometres to get back to their owner's house."

"*Dogs* do that," Alfreeda said. "Some walk for *hundreds* of kilometres. They're so brave."

I wanted to shout, "How can you brag about dogs at a time like this?" But Grandma Kit was already outside, looking for Darcy. I ran after her, and Alfreeda ran after me.

We looked behind the chicken coop. We checked between hay bales. We looked in trees.

"He's not in the farmyard," Grandma Kit said at last. "He'd be crying in this rain, for sure. Come on, girls."

All three of us piled into the truck and headed up the road towards town. Grandma Kit turned the headlights on high. They lit up the road. She drove very slowly.

"Alfreeda, you watch the left side of the road," she said. "You watch the right, Tabitha."

We peered out of the windows. Rain came down in grey sheets. The sky was almost as dark as night. Thunder began to rumble.

"What if we can't find him?" Alfreeda asked. "Joy will never see him again. If I lost my best friend in a pouring rainstorm while I was lying in a hospital, I'd be sad forever."

Grandma Kit didn't say anything. She just patted Alfreeda's knee.

We reached town, and Grandma Kit drove up and down the streets. Before long, she stopped the truck. She turned off the engine and pointed at a small house.

"That's the Jacksons' home," she said. "Look who's there."

"Darcy!" I cried, throwing open the truck door and leaping out.

I ran to the front steps of the Jacksons' house and gathered Darcy in my arms. He was muddy, crying, shivering and dripping wet.

I raced him to the truck and laid him in Alfreeda's lap. I took off my raincoat and sweater, then wrapped the sweater around him.

"He must've run like the wind to get here so quickly," Grandma Kit said. "I better call Joy's parents and tell them what happened."

She called Ms Jackson.

"Annie, I'm so sorry, but Darcy escaped from Tabby Towers and ran home," Grandma Kit said.

"I'm not surprised, Kit," Ms Jackson said. "Joy is just as unhappy without him. She's so sad. I don't think being apart from her sweet, furry friend is good for her weak heart."

"We're on our way," Grandma Kit said. She didn't wait for Ms Jackson's reply. She hung up and started the truck. Then she zoomed through the thunderstorm towards the city, an hour's drive away.

⇒CHAPTER 6⇐
The secret plan

The heavy rain and dark clouds made it hard for Grandma Kit to see the road.

"Driving in thunderstorms always makes me nervous," she said. "I wish Scruffy were here. That cat would sit on my lap the whole way and keep me calm."

She turned on the radio. Soft music played.

Alfreeda and I took turns holding and petting Darcy. At last, he stopped shivering. He lay still and quiet in my arms.

We began to see the bright lights of the city. Grandma Kit found the hospital and parked the truck. Then we headed inside.

The waiting area on the main floor was full of people. I kept Darcy wrapped in the sweater.

"Looks like you're holding a baby," Alfreeda whispered in my ear.

Grandma Kit called Ms Jackson. A few minutes later, she came to meet us.

"Here, Ms Jackson," I said, offering Darcy to her. She shook her head at me, then looked at Grandma Kit.

"I tried calling you back," Ms Jackson said. "Your ringer must've been turned off. I asked the nurse if Darcy could visit Joy. The answer was no. He said pets weren't allowed."

"But we *have* to get Darcy upstairs to Joy," I said. "He will make her feel so much better."

Then I saw it: a sign on a door that said, *MOTHER-BABY CENTRE*. The door led to the hospital's birthing unit. I noticed a box of lost-and-found items beside the door too.

I had an idea. A good one. A top-secret one.

A hospital guard sat at the welcome desk. He wasn't looking in the direction of the box. I quietly handed Darcy to Alfreeda and whispered, "I have a plan. But I'll need your help, okay? I'll be right back."

I hurried to the box and dug through the stuff. I took two things and hurried back to the others.

"Come here," I whispered, leading them behind a few tall plants.

I showed everyone the baby hat and baby blanket I'd taken from the box. Alfreeda grinned and took the sweater off Darcy.

She put the baby hat on his head. It fitted him purr-fectly and looked *so* cute.

Next, I wrapped the baby blanket around him. I covered his whole body. Just the top of his hat and the tiniest bit of his face showed.

I laid Darcy in Ms Jackson's arms. He went totally limp, like a sleeping baby. He didn't make a sound.

"Hey, it looks like you're cradling a real baby," Alfreeda said.

"I bet it will fool the guard," I said. "Take Darcy upstairs to Joy's room, okay? No one will know."

Ms Jackson looked at Grandma Kit. Grandma Kit shrugged at her and smiled.

"All right," Ms Jackson whispered. "I'll go along with the plan. Anything to cheer up Joy. Darcy is the only one who can make her feel better right now."

"Can we come?" Alfreeda asked. "I know Joy from school. I bet she'd like to meet Tabby Cat too."

"Of course," Ms Jackson said.

"You run along. I'll stay here," Grandma Kit said. "I need to call Tom and see how the other kitties are doing."

Ms Jackson, Darcy, Alfreeda and I moved towards the hospital guard. I held my breath.

CHAPTER 7
The wrapped surprise

We sailed right past the hospital guard. Easy! He was busy talking to a woman in a wheelchair. He didn't even notice the "baby" in Ms Jackson's arms.

The lift bell dinged, and the door opened. A nurse stood inside.

Uh-oh, I thought.

Ms Jackson walked into the lift. Alfreeda and I followed.

"What floor would you like?" the nurse asked.

"Fifth floor, please," Ms Jackson said.

"Certainly," the nurse said. She pressed the fifth-floor button. The lift began to move upwards. "May I see your baby?"

I gulped. My heart started to pound. Alfreeda's eyes grew to twice their usual size.

"I'm sorry," Ms Jackson said in a kind voice. "My daughter is very ill. It's best if others don't come too close. You understand."

"Of course, of course," the nurse said, giving Ms Jackson a sad smile. "You've come to the right place. We'll take good care of your daughter here."

"Thank you," Ms Jackson said.

The lift door opened. Ms Jackson walked quickly down the corridor towards Joy's room. Alfreeda and I rushed behind her.

And then, there we were, inside Joy's room. She lay in bed, wearing a hospital robe. Her father sat in a chair beside her. He was holding her hand.

Ms Jackson shut the door behind us and cried, "We did it! Thank you, girls!" She sat next to Joy on the bed and laid the wrapped surprise beside her. "Look, Joy," Ms Jackson said. "Take off the blanket."

Joy peeled the blanket away and gasped. Darcy saw her and began to meow.

"My Darcy," Joy cried. She cradled him and gave him a bunch of nose kisses.

Darcy raised his front legs and wrapped them around Joy's neck.

"Look! He's *hugging* you," Alfreeda said in a shocked voice. "Wow. I never knew cats hugged their people."

"Darcy always hugs me," Joy said.

I couldn't believe my eyes either. It was an actual hug. It seemed like Darcy was trying to make his sick best friend feel better.

Just then, the door opened, and a nurse walked in. He looked at Joy, then at Darcy. His mouth fell open.

"How did that muddy cat get in here?" he asked. "No, no, no. It better leave the way it came. Right now!"

CHAPTER 8
The purr-fect plan

Joy started to cry. She cried really hard.

The nurse raced to her side. "Calm down, calm down," he said. "It's very bad for your heart to get this upset."

Joy kept on crying. "Don't take Darcy away," she said. "I'm scared here, and Darcy makes me less scared."

"Shhh," the nurse said, patting her arm. "Okay, Darcy can stay for a little while."

"How long?" Joy asked, crying less hard now.

"We'll see," the nurse said. "Stop those tears now. That's a good girl. We need you to stay calm, okay? I'm going to check your heart rate. Then I'll take your blood pressure."

Joy stopped crying. She rubbed her face in Darcy's fur. She closed her eyes and patted his back. The room became very quiet.

The nurse checked Joy's heart rate and blood pressure. He looked surprised, then wrote the numbers on a clipboard.

The door opened again, and this time Joy's doctor marched in.

"Hello, everyone," she said. "How's our brave girl doing on her big day?"

She looked at Joy, and her smile quickly turned to a frown.

"How did that dirty cat get in here?" she said. "No pets are allowed in the hospital."

"Doctor?" the nurse said. "Look at this." He held out the clipboard. "Joy's heart rate and blood pressure are *lower* now than when she arrived this morning."

"That's because Darcy's here," I spoke up. "It's true. My grandma always says that her cat, Scruffy, calms her down. Pets can make their owners healthier."

Joy looked at the doctor. "I *need* Darcy here," she said. "He's already making me feel better. Can he stay? Please?"

The doctor sighed. Finally, she said, "All right. But someone needs to give him a bath."

"I will," I offered.

"I'll help," Alfreeda said.

I carried Darcy to the sink in Joy's small bathroom. Alfreeda and I gave him a quick soapy bath and dried him with a towel.

A few minutes later, we carried him back out. He looked like his old self again.

"That's the most beautiful cat I've ever seen," said the nurse.

"You *are* a handsome one," the doctor said to Darcy, scratching him under the chin. "You take good care of Joy now, okay?"

"Meow," Darcy said.

I laid Darcy beside Joy. She smiled happily, and Darcy purred.

🐾 🐾 🐾

Before long, Ms Jackson took Alfreeda and me back to the waiting room.

"Darcy's my hero," I said. "He knows exactly how to make Joy feel better."

"That's not a true hero," Alfreeda said. "Dogs that save people's lives — *they're* heroes."

Ms Jackson cleared her throat. "Alfreeda?" she said. "I'm going to tell you a true story. A week ago, Darcy started acting strangely. He wouldn't stop pawing at Joy's chest and crying. I'd read many real-life stories about cats that had discovered their owners' illnesses."

The lift reached the main floor, and we stepped out. Ms Jackson finished her story in the corridor.

"So, I took Joy to the clinic," she said. "The doctor ran some tests. We were shocked. Joy had a bad heart! We were lucky we found out when we did. Joy was supposed to have gone to football camp this week. The doctor said the exercise could've caused Joy's heart to stop."

"Oh," Alfreeda said.

"Mm-hmm," said Ms Jackson. "Darcy is a hero. Without question, he saved Joy's life. Many cats have saved people's lives."

Alfreeda nodded.

I smiled. For once, Alfreeda had nothing to say, and that was great.

❖ ❖ ❖

The sun shone brightly through the big windows in the hospital waiting room. The storm had passed.

Ms Jackson talked quietly to Grandma Kit for a minute, then it was time to go. Alfreeda and I said goodbye to Ms Jackson. She thanked us about five times for bringing Darcy to the hospital to visit Joy.

"We'll have to work quickly when we get home," I said, walking to the truck. "It's almost time for the magic show."

"Mmm," Grandma Kit said. She didn't say a word as we drove through the city.

"Is something wrong?" I asked.

"Yes, I'm afraid so," she said. "Mr and Ms Jackson have to stay in a hotel while Joy is in the hospital. And they both have to miss many days of work. They will have a lot of bills to pay when they go back home."

We drove in silence for a while. I thought hard, wondering how I could help the Jackson family. I kept thinking about how cute Darcy looked too, in that pink baby hat.

Then I got an idea. A purr-fect one.

"We'll do another fundraiser!" I said. "All the money we earn can go to the Jacksons. This time, we'll have a kitty fashion show!"

Alfreeda looked at me and grinned. "That's a great idea," she said. "I love it! I'll totally help. I'll draw some cute clothes the kitties can wear: hats, dresses, coats . . ."

"Could you sew them, Grandma Kit?" I asked.

"I'd be happy to," she said.

"Darcy is so laid-back, we can dress him in baby clothes," Alfreeda went on. "And push him in a pushchair during the show."

"Well, I think Darcy should wear *superhero* clothes, don't you?" I asked. "As he's such a hero?"

Alfreeda was quiet for a moment. "Yeah, you're right, Tabby Cat," she said. "Superhero clothes would be perfect for Darcy. He should definitely have a cape."

My head was spinning with ideas now. "Grandpa Tom can build a long, fancy catwalk," I said. "The kitties will walk down it, modelling the clothes. We'll have music and lights too. Just like in a real fashion show."

"We'll put an advert in the newspaper," Alfreeda said. "We'll get the whole town to come. We'll give the Jacksons front-row seats."

"We can start telling people about it at the magic show this afternoon," I said.

Grandma Kit grinned. "There's paper and a pen in my purse, girls," she said. "You better get started on those clothes."

I dug in the purse, found the paper and pen, and handed them to Alfreeda. She began to draw.

"I hope Joy will be well enough to come," I said.

"Oh, I bet she will be," Grandma Kit said. "This fundraiser is going to make her so happy. Her parents too."

"Nothing feels better than making other people happy," I said.

"That's for sure," said Alfreeda. "Even a *cat* knows that."

I laughed and watched Alfreeda draw cute kitty fashions the whole way home.

Is a Ragdoll
the cat for you?

Hello, it's me, Tabitha!

I bet you'd LOVE your own sweet, beautiful ragdoll cat now, right? I completely understand. Ragdolls make great pets for families with kids. Actually, ragdolls are a good fit for almost any home. Here's why:

First, ragdolls are friendly. They can get along with all kinds of people and pets, including dogs. Second, ragdolls are calm and gentle. They're not big jumpers, and they play without sticking out their claws. And third, they're not hard to train.

But before you buy or adopt one, there are some important things you should know:

Ragdolls are long-haired cats that must be brushed every day. Their undercoats mat easily. Matted hair irritates cats. Also, brushing often will stop your ragdoll getting hairballs. (Cats groom themselves by licking their fur. They swallow hair, which forms a ball in their stomachs. Large hairballs can be deadly for cats.)

Ragdolls have a high rate of heart problems. It's important that ragdoll owners plan regular check-ups with a vet.

Ragdolls should be kept indoors. They're peaceful cats, not born fighters. If another animal attacks them, they won't fight back. Ragdolls also don't seem to care about hunting. They're happy to live inside, where they're safe.

All right, cat lovers! That's all for now . . . until the next adventure at Tabby Towers!

Meowingly yours,

Tabitha Catarina Felinus (Tabby Cat, for short)

Glossary

annoying making someone feel angry or impatient

blood pressure force of blood as it flows through a person's body; a blood pressure test tells how hard and fast a person's heart is beating

fundraiser event that brings in money for a cause or project

hairball ball of fur that lodges in a cat's stomach; hairballs are made of fur swallowed by a cat as it cleans itself

heart rate number of heartbeats in a given time, usually a minute

operation medical treatment where the body is cut open

selfish caring only about oneself, not others

shiver tremble

social enjoying the company of others

vet doctor who cares for animals

Talk about it

1. Alfreeda says that cats care only about themselves. But that doesn't seem to be true in Darcy's case. Share examples from the story that suggest Darcy cares a great deal about Joy.

2. Look at the illustration on page 37 and describe what's happening in this part of the story. Why do the two girls look so surprised?

3. On page 66, Tabby Cat has shared some facts about ragdoll cats. Do you think a ragdoll would be a good cat for your family? Why or why not?

Write about it

1. Write a newspaper advert that tells readers about the kitty fashion show. It should include details about what people will see if they attend and where the fundraiser money will go.

2. The kitty fashion show was a hit! Pretend you're Joy and write a letter to everyone at Tabby Towers. Thank them for the fundraiser and for bringing Darcy to the hospital.

3. Write a one-page essay on ragdoll cats. Make sure you use at least three sources.

About the author

Shelley Swanson Sateren has been a freelance writer for thirty years and has written more than forty books for children, both fiction and non-fiction. As well as writing, Shelley has worked as a children's book editor and in a children's bookshop. She is also a primary school teacher and has enjoyed employment in several schools. Shelley lives in Minnesota, USA, with her husband and has two grown-up sons.

About the illustrator

Deborah Melmon has worked as an illustrator for more than twenty-five years. After graduating from Academy of Art University in San Francisco, she started her career illustrating covers for the *Palo Alto Weekly* newspaper. Since then, she has produced artwork for more than twenty children's books. Her artwork can also be found on wrapping paper, greeting cards and fabric. Deborah lives in California, USA, and shares her studio with an energetic Airedale Terrier called Mack.

VISIT
TABBY TOWERS
AGAIN WITH
THESE AWESOME
ADVENTURES!

ADVENTURES at
TABBY TOWERS
Leaping
Lizzie

Queen Lizzie's Pizza Palace

Written by
...mson Sateren

Illustrated by
Deborah Melmon

ADVENTURES at
TABBY TOWERS
Boxing
Bootsie

Written by
Shelley Swanson Sateren

Illustrated by
Deborah Melmon

ADVENTURES at
TABBY TOWERS
Disappearing
Darcy

Written by
Shelley Swanson Sateren

Illustrated by
Deborah Melmon

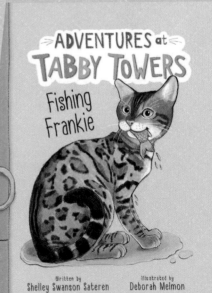

ADVENTURES at
TABBY TOWERS
Fishing
Frankie

Written by
Shelley Swanson Sateren

Illustrated by
Deborah Melmon

(WE PROMISED ALFREEDA
WE'D INCLUDE THE
HOUND HOTEL GUESTS
AND THEIR SUPER-FUN
STORIES HERE TOO!)

www.raintree.co.uk